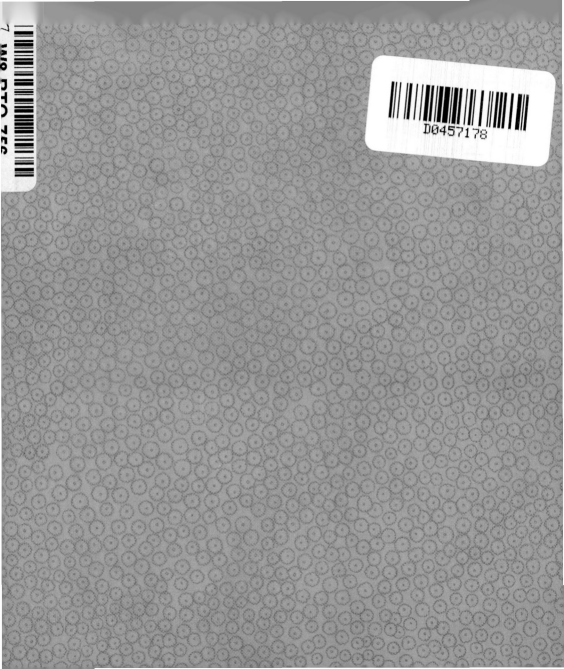

JONATHAN SMALL
AND ELIZABETH BLUE

A Friendship Story
By Dean Walley
Illustrated by Merrily Johnson

HALLMARK CHILDREN'S EDITIONS

Jonathan Small and Elizabeth Blue

Jonathan Small was lonely. He didn't have any friends to play with.

Elizabeth Blue was lonely, too.
She didn't have any friends to play with, either.

They might have been friends with each other.
But Jonathan Small lived on one side of a big hill.

And Elizabeth Blue lived on the other side.
That's why they hadn't met—at least not yet.

One day they both decided to go exploring. They were tired of playing in their own yards with their own toys and their own tricycles. They wanted to find out what the world was like. And they wanted to find some friends.

So Jonathan Small took his hat from the hall and his glove and his ball, and away he went.

Elizabeth Blue picked a dress that was new and her favorite shoes, and away she went, too.

Jonathan Small walked a long, long way. Then he walked some more. Soon he got tired. So he sat down beside a big tree to rest.

"Hello, big tree. You don't know me," said Jonathan Small.

Then the branches of the tree began to rustle in the wind and the tree seemed to say, over and over and over again, "I'm your friend. I'm your friend."

Jonathan Small didn't know what to think about that. He decided he liked the tree. Before he left to explore some more, he said, "Goodbye, Mr. Tree. You've been nice to me. I'm glad you're my friend. Hope we meet again."

You remember Elizabeth Blue. She'd gone exploring, too. And she walked and she walked and she walked. Then she got tired. So she sat down beside a little brook to rest.

Elizabeth was very surprised when the brook seemed to say in a watery way, "I'm your friend the brook. How pretty you look. I'm your friend the brook. How pretty you look."

Now Elizabeth Blue didn't know what to think of that. But she looked into the water. And who do you think she saw? Elizabeth Blue! She looked pretty, too.

That made her feel very happy. Soon she was ready to explore some more. But before she did, she said, "Goodbye, Mr. Brook. I'm glad you're my friend. Before very long, I'll see you again."

About that time, Jonathan Small, who had found no friends at all (except for the tree) had walked to a place where the buildings were tall. He was lost. He didn't know where to go.

Just then a policeman came walking by.

"What's your name, young man?" asked the policeman.

"I'm Jonathan Small. I can't find any friends at all, except for the tree."

"Well, what about me?" said the policeman.

"You mean you're my friend?" said Jonathan Small to the policeman, who seemed about seven feet tall.

"Of course I'm your friend. And I want to help you if I can," said the policeman.

Jonathan Small was so happy when he heard this that he jumped up and down and laughed like a clown and ran on his way without hearing what else his new friend had to say.

At that very moment, Elizabeth Blue got a rock in her shoe. And it hurt! So she sat on the sidewalk and started to cry. Just then a lady came by. She was a nurse who was dressed all in white. She stopped to see if things were all right.

"What's your name, little girl?" asked the nurse. "Is anything wrong?"

"I'm Elizabeth Blue," said Elizabeth Blue. "I can't find a friend, except for the brook, and something is terribly wrong with my shoe! Could you take a look?"

Inside the shoe of Elizabeth Blue, tucked inside the sock, the nurse found the rock. She took it out and threw it away. Then she said, "I'm your friend, Elizabeth."

That made Elizabeth Blue so happy that she jumped up and down and danced all around and shouted, "Hooray!" and ran on her way.

Meanwhile, our friend, Jonathan Small, had run from the place where the buildings were tall to a place where there weren't any buildings at all.

He was more lost than ever. He wished he had stayed with his friend, the policeman.

Just then a little gray dog came by. He looked very sad. Jonathan thought he looked lost, too. Jonathan wanted to help him.

"Cheer up, little dog," said Jonathan Small. "We'll find our way home in no time at all. You're my puppy now and I'll call you Paul."

When he heard that, the pup cheered up.

"The top of the hill seems the best place to me to find the way home. Don't you agree?" said Jonathan Small.

Paul wagged his tail as little dogs will, which meant, "I agree! Let's climb up the hill." So they did.

While on her way home, Elizabeth Blue had gone the wrong way. Now she was lost, too! And she wished she had stayed with her new friend, the nurse.

But a kitten she met made her forget about being sad. She even felt glad.

"I think you're lost, too," said Elizabeth Blue to the cat she named Sue. "But we both can be found if we just look around." And the two of them started climbing the hill.

Well, Jonathan Small and his friend, Paul, and Elizabeth Blue and her friend, Sue, reached the top of the hill at exactly the same time.

"Hello. How are you?" said Elizabeth Blue.

"I'm fine. This is Paul," said Jonathan Small.

And they began telling each other about the things that they had found and the friends they had made while they wandered around.

"Can I be your friend, too?" asked Elizabeth Blue.

"You can be my best friend of all!" said Jonathan Small.

They were so happy they completely forgot about being lost. But, as it turned out, they weren't really lost at all, for when they looked down the hill, they could see their houses below.

They agreed they would meet and play together often, and then they went home.

The mother and dad of Jonathan Small were happy to see him. They let him keep Paul. And the mother and dad of Elizabeth Blue were happy to see her, too, and they let her keep Sue.

And now, after making so many friends, Elizabeth Blue and Jonathan Small are never, ever lonely at all.

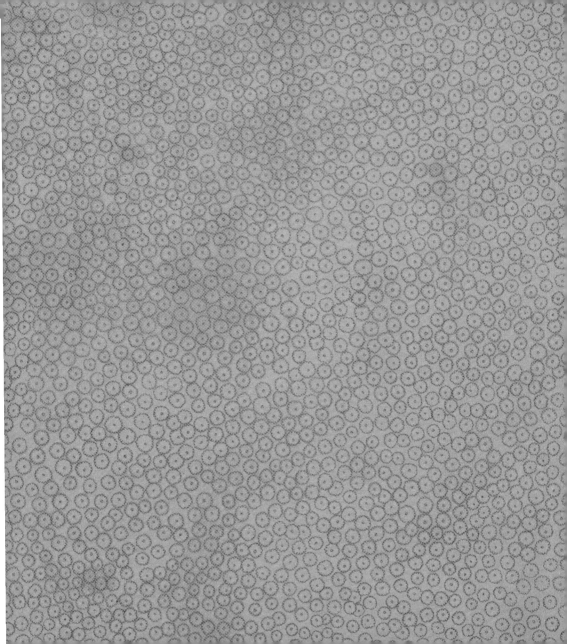